# at the beach

BY ANNE ROCKWELL     ILLUSTRATED BY HARLOW ROCKWELL

ALADDIN · New York · London · Toronto · Sydney · New Delhi

❧ ALADDIN

An imprint of Simon & Schuster Children's Publishing Division
1230 Avenue of the Americas, New York, NY 10020
This Aladdin hardcover edition June 2014
Copyright © 1987 by Anne Rockwell and Harlow Rockwell
Front jacket illustration copyright © 2014 by Lizzy Rockwell
All other jacket illustrations copyright © 1987 by Harlow Rockwell
For information about special discounts for bulk purchases, please contact Simon & Schuster
Special Sales at 1-866-506-1949 or business@simonandschuster.com.
The Simon & Schuster Speakers Bureau can bring authors to your live event. For more
information or to book an event contact the Simon & Schuster Speakers Bureau at
1-866-248-3049 or visit our website at www.simonspeakers.com.
Designed by Jessica Handelman
The text of this book was set in Kindergarten.
Manufactured in China 0314 SCP
10 9 8 7 6 5 4 3 2 1
Library of Congress Cataloging-in-Publication Data
Rockwell, Anne F.
At the beach / Anne & Harlow Rockwell.—1st Aladdin Books ed.
p. cm.
Summary: A child experiences an enjoyable day at the beach
[1. Beaches—Fiction.] 1. Rockwell, Harlow. II. Title.
PZ7.R5943Atm   1991
[E]—dc20   90-45620   CIP   AC
ISBN 978-1-4814-1133-2 (hc)
ISBN 978-1-4814-1401-2 (eBook)

I wear my bathing suit
and I bring my shovel and pail
when I go to the beach.

We bring our towels
and beach umbrella
and tote bag with us.

In the tote bag
there are two cups
and a thermos of lemonade.

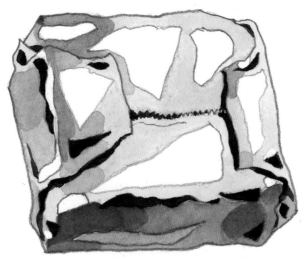

We have two sandwiches
wrapped in aluminum foil
and two peaches for lunch.

There is a tube of sunscreen
to rub on our skin
so we don't get sunburned.
I like the way
the sunscreen smells.

Little sandpipers run
down the beach
and I follow them.

My feet make footprints
in the wet sand.
The sandpipers make footprints, too.

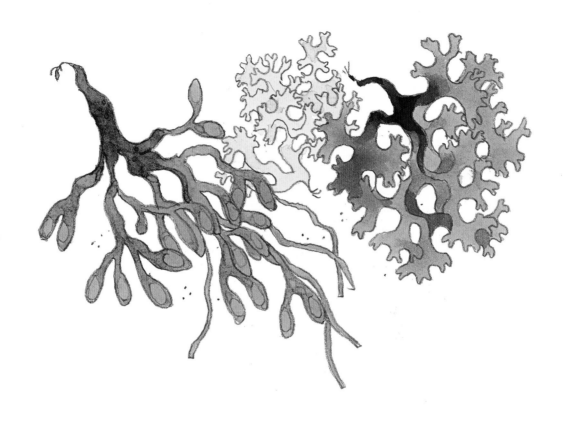

I find some seaweed

and seashells on the beach.

I build a castle with my shovel and pail.
The boy next to me digs a channel
where his boat can float.

Everyone is building something
in the sand at the beach.

I wade in the water.
A little crab tweaks my toe,
and little silver fishes
swim past me.

I like to walk
past the lifeguard's station
to the big, brown rocks.

That is where the barnacles
and snails and mussels live.

When my mother and I go swimming,
the waves crash on us
and get us all wet.
A big sea gull swims close to us.

Then I lie on my towel
and dry myself in the hot sun
until it is time . . .

for lunch.